BOY TAIL
a fable

John Moletress

©2017, JM, all rights reserved

1.
Like sand sharks
And velvet dresses
To the South, smoothing water
To the North, cat tongue

A boy at a beach house,
who shall be called Boy.

2.
Odontaspididae,
Shiver of hunters,
Gulpers of air

At the beach rental house,
Boy arranges meat flowers,
a sand shark bouquet,
strewn upon wooden railing,
three in a row.

Boy plays boat Captain,
who plays Ginger after midnight,
makes wigs of bleached coral,
jellyfish,
and sand shell keychains.

On the boat Dirty Jerzey,
floating on the bay,
uncle daddies lead games,
which boy's breath was held longest.

Decent daddies were old Saint Nicks,
didn't keep receipts.

So, begins,
Boy's sensual gifts,
pirate's booty,
fisherman's plunder,
beasts of the sea.

The trainee twink,
snatches the yellow pail,

filled with an inch of sea,
tosses in sand sharks,
1, 2, 3.

3.
Velvet sharks can grow at horse's length,
But Boy's sharks remained average for men.

Lacan

Mother in the kitchen.

Mother in the kitchen,
spreading Hellman's.

Spreads it on
THICK
Meier's Italian bread.

Follows:

>three slices of ham
>two slices of white American
>deli cheese
>one slice tomato
>one tear
>>from mother's garden
>>secret.

4.
Could sharks survive
in sunlight
without water?

White hot Boardwalk summer,
Helios' red stilettos,
tramping on shark's backs.

Baking
dancin' the Hot Railin'
ocean city potato
chip lips
vinegar wounds

At a time somewhere between starboard and house, the sharks stopped moving.

Boy is a curious child.

Just yesterday…
    brought back blue balls
    from staring at
    blue crabs

    annnnnd…
        brought back a crab
        dancin' the Crab Walk Prance
        in the beach house backyard

        Boy found a hammer
            (in his father daddy's jeep)
        to bring down upon crab
        to see its insides

Christmas Eve, 1985

Boy, at bar stool height,
made chocolate chip cookies
to serve to bloated Santa, *to rub*
who carried stems of rosebuds, *on his cock*
and lactose intolerance.

On the eve of the babe's barn birth,
a celebration of Barbra Streisand's early albums,
uncles, aunties and non-consensual cousins,
shoveled pink crab meat down gullets,
wiped mouths with new golf clubs,
licked the living room television,
which played something called football.

Secret cousin Maddie jigged the dirty grin on a pear-shaped frame.

Secret cousin Maddie had a dirty brain six years older than Boy.

Secret cousin Maddie grabbed Boy's hand with butter fingers to lead Boy upstairs.

And

6.
THIS PAGE IS "INTENTIONALLY" LEFT BLANK

> 7.
> *Cat's tongue is coarse,*
> *Wet-dry.*

Boy, the curiosity,
and the anxiety,
of a diabetic cat.

Boy runs fingers
across gender,
sand shark grey,
because gender unknown,
because sharks.

Boy had no aptitude for biology.
He knew multitudes of show tunes.

Headz2tailz,
a boy band of sand sharks,
bake in the haze
of the dying sun.

At the Captured Sand Shark Please Touch Museum:

> Electrical thrills through Boy flesh,
> fireworks spreading through space folliculitis.
> Boy desperately wishes for arm hair,
> the thicket most desirable in circles of boys.

> Bumps rise on skin send head back priest-throat
> hands on neck Boy experiences Helios retina spells
> witchcraft sending Boy at now and present to then
> and there and then to locker room flood lamps
> swaying above shin-high benches and the balls cage,
> the cage he's in, wolves and spiders and bears.

       Mr. Pennypacker: "Boy, you must shower."
       Boy: (sneaks out)

This is a scene made for a light dance

On the track field,
Boy practices lessons,
learned of great illusionists,
by disappearing like vapor,
under bleachers.

Twirling spaghetti grass,
between finger and thumb,
Boy squints, contorts eyes
towards other boy's legs.

Winged Mercury,
bodies carried on carbon,
around and around,
the dirty brown loop.

On the track field,
candy and peach schnapps legs,
intoxicate athleticism.

Boy pierces with a stare,
asses of pre-soldiering Romans,
butt bubbling under Op's,
of arrows and Saint Sebastian.

Hair lip French fries,
(human fryolator),
boys' hair cooks by sun,
expels scents of boy body.

Boy commands his own
legs sprout moss,

fresh carpet.

It was not yet that boy may realize a future in which the slapping of his legs forcefully with own hands may be turned transactional potential for daddies who lick lips; an obsession of crisp pain.

8.
I'll name the shark, Drew.
But the shark
mustn't be named.

Drew
Drew?
DREW.
DDRREEWW!

(if "I" were here, "i" would have a bubble heart)

> 9.
> *Drew*
> *Track all-star*
> *Populist*
> *Everyman*
> *Tan*
> *Drew*

THIS IS AN EXERCISE

Close your eyes.

Close them.

Real tiiight.

Now:

Manifest your greatest infatuation,
the one you'd drown in piss for,
pluck out your heart with antique figurine,
eat your own tongue.

CLOSE YOUR EYES,
so, say I.

Count backwards from ten.

Slowly.

YOU LOSE!   YOU TOUCHED YOURSELF!
             YOU TOUCHED YOURSELF!
             YOU TOUCHED YOURSELF!
             YOU TOUCHED YOURSELF!
HA! HA!   YOU TOUCHED YOURSELF!
LOSER.

THIS IS NOT AN EXERCISE
                    anymore.

Drew walked the peculiar wide road gait,
best described as holding a basketball by one's taint,
as one may do for a blue ribbon on Field Day.

In Pennsylvanian winters, Drew remained tan.

Rarely, he gestured,
unlike Boy,
whose limbs operated,
by fairy remote,
oft dancing in moonlight,
and motion sensor light,
on the shadows of deer.

Drew's dead carp arms,
lifeless at his sides.

    D-iwantu-R-iwanna-E-withinme-W-4ever!

Even when signaling his minions, Drew sprang claws from morphing hands, into track captain hooks, snarled his upper lip to nose, furrowed the brow into singular formation, the topography of the Pocono Mountains, the mythical manly werewolf.

10.
sand sharks have guts the size of

Run, Boy, run,
sounds the class warning bell,
from the bowels of aluminum bleachers,
to the locker room,
fastest mile of the day.

> So, so fast to beat the track stars so he may get
> dressed as to hide his own body from the repeal of...
>
> TIGGER WARNING: the hopping up and down

Boy never touched an incident without a fly swatter
Boy really, really, really wanted scars
and hairy legs
> DO YOU REMEMBER
> THE TIME WHEN
> PUNCTUATION BETRAYED?

Often.
other boys.
would find displeasure.
with Boy's clothing)
as if taking personal offense;
in boi* fashion!

Boy buckled,
imperfect weight,
the excess belly,
the soft, undefined chest,
inadequate growth,
thickening ankles.

Boy felt more peach than boy.

11.
red belongs on whore curtains

"DO NOT SPILL ANYTHING ON THE COUCH!"

Boy was warned,
by Mother.

After school,
Boy walks two miles home,
a safety of avoidance,
spinning Reebok tracks like Charlotte's web,
suburbia's winding back roads snake,
cul de sacs of paper dolls,
ranchers made of
proverbs and glass

              gray   ecru
              beige sand
              occasionally, umber

SYMBOLS FOR SALE!
by Tammi and Ted and Savannah and Steven and Bobbi and Bobby Polish surnames

2:58	BOY HOME ALONE
2:59	CLICK ON TV
3:00	MAKE PEANUT BUTTER & JELLY ON MAIER'S ITALIAN BREAD
3:03-3:55	WATCH GENERAL HOSPITAL
3:55-4:00	STARE OUT THE WINDOW
4:00-4:50	OPRAH!
4:50	MOTHER ENTERS
4:51	MOTHER CRIES
4:53	MOTHER ON TOILET

```
4:56        MOTHER NOT ON TOILET
4:55        MOTHER FEEDS A BLIND CAT
4:57        MOTHER CRIES
4:59        MOTHER MAKES EARL GREY
5:00        MOTHER STARES AT THE WALL, SIPPING TEA
```

Mother grips,
claws at the order of things,
a mysterious play book,
shifting ideologies,
that only she knew.

In 1983,
mother made a bed for father
on the downstairs couch.

In 1993,
he remained.

Mother made it a mission,
to control what she could,
the keeping of objects,
at store-bought newness
well past their relevancy.

Mother keeps things,
Tupperware full of receipts.

Instead they remain,
as ungiven gifts
on basement shelves.

Mother soldiered with friends Windex and Bounty.

After dinner,
boy in his room,
lined with wallpaper,

toy trucks, trains and sports.

Boy wonders if his parents know him at all.

Under the bed,
Boy kept a notebook,
of big time Broadway!

That's where,
he etched his name,
prominently above,
the show's title.

In dreaming,
Boy played Grizabella,
wrapped in grandmother's furs,
moping and
weeping and
belting
high notes to pussycats.

See Boy on the balcony,
the Casa de Rosado?

Dislocating his arms,
towards the shirtless,
and racially miscast,
chorus boys below.

Deep in the intestines,
of the Paris Opera House,
on a boat commandeered,
by a songstress half-masc,
Boy discovers the brutality,
of eight shows a week.

12.
Stella made

O, Stella!

Witch churning
butter and flour.

Boo-boo grandmom,
she was nicknamed.

> The culinary queen of St. Pius X High!
> Manager of Macaroni and Cheese!
> Supervisor of Children's Appetites!
> Boiler Maker!

Her throne,
> Queen of Chickens and Jesus Princesses!

a small office tucked away,
behind black oil fryolators,
baking machines,
the city of Industry,
and oeuvre of scorched cheese.

In her chamber,
a savage machine,
brushed gun metal beast,
chipping turquoise paint,
purposed to organize milk money
into bank sleeves,
oft spitting coins,
where they didn't belong.

Uncivil machine,
RATTLER!

CONVULSER!
legs chained to the wall.
Power up,
see Boy feel
agitating cylinders,
push pennies, dimes, half dollars,
an occasional buffalo nickel,
which would send the metal beast,
into fits.

If only, Boy thought, existence could have such meaning!

Violence finds comfort,
the putting of things in place,
taken after his Mother, surely.

Boo-boo, first generation immigrant, baked crumb apple pies in the apple salvage yard, heaping mounds of cinnamon, both white and brown Domino's. A slice explodes at the touch, a water park slide.

> INTOXIFY
> INTOXICATE
> INTOXICATION

Boo-boo pie,
Grand art,
Revolution!
Long live mouth ecstasy!

Intermediate states,
the Bardo Pennsylvania,
each taste bud mutating,
shape-shifting pinball machine.

Pairs well with Thanksgiving,
tryptophan anarchy,
counter criminal activity,

reviving misfit children from fowl coma.

Boo-boo,
adorned in caftans,
purple and red,
cuts,
scars,
fights,
with steel cutlery,
cooking oil,
making Easter patterns
on overcast farms.

    and then...

Retiring home, a perpendicular half block down American Street, was where she styled entries in a three by five notebook, the diary of daily living, spattered with marinara and beef stock. A life found its home among recipes for French dressing, potato salad and green beans with lard and bacon, peppered with doctor's appointments, home repairs and the death of Mickey, the diabetic terrier.

13.
The secret garden of the Mary child

Outside Stella's chamber door, where fryers went to die and the kitchen's service entrance, lived a splashy, aluminum spaceship, the stuff of war bunkers of era's before, complete with mechanical, weaponized latch.

DEEP FREEZER

Boy tucks low, makes himself feral around hidden flour corners, observes the ladies' home journal hair net parade, marching billows of thick, magic smoke, returning with a newborn, suckling pig.

Adventure was Boy's sport.
He makes himself available for play.

Boy puts an ear to the spatial ship door.

Listening

Come in
whispered a

voice

                          Come in
                                          from inside the
          spaceship

                            Come
                                        and so

Boy sneaks from his hiding,
looks three times,
coast is clear,
grabs the latch.
       tugging
              Is anyone watching?
       pulling

       engulfed by myth smoke

                      now inside.

Deep freezer mystery,
 surprising
atmosphere,
lung-breathing,
       (no allergies to ice)
but not earth-like,
cauterizing nose,
Copperfield hatch,
creeping out the world,
the door shuts,
trapping Boy inside.

       blue
       blue packages
       blue peas carrots corn
       blue metal
            and noise, blue
            blueness

>   fingers, blue
> *into blue*
> *into blue*
>   glide to stick
>   cracking
>   packages

Boy gingerly/thrashing/curdling ghost ship electro-pop techno 120 bpm crackle of singing soups stews sides burgeoning rituals

Captain Boo-boo
absent alchemist
where are the spoons
for stirring communal cauldrons?

Sorceress of the Floral Sundays!

Swimming deeper into the frozen ocean, a chamber door appears as secret within secret.

> *Boy loves mystery stories.*
> *Chose adventures by owning them.*
> *Boy thinks this house is haunted by his former inability to move.*

He binds hands in a Hanes t-shirt, tugs at the small door, to guide, to ride, to slide in.

This was easier than he imagined.

XIII.
Within
Breath

Come closer

                                            Where?

Come closer

                                            I do not see
                                            you

I am here

                                            Where is?

Right in front of you

                                            The room is dark
                                            Too dark to see
                                            you
                                            What are you?

breath
breathing

I am strange
and familiar
I am kind
and unkind
I am the bewilderment,
the fragmented
I am the dark
and the things,

taken from innocence

                                                Have you?

Been waiting

                                                My shoes are
                                                made of ice,
                                                not for running
                                                away

This place/road,
slippery

I am the tall figure/   Are you a beast?
I gulp surface air
move on the back of stillness
like the sand shark
that hunts in shivers

Closer/   Do you hunt?
Closer/   Do you hunt
now?
Closer/   Are you?

silently on the imperceptible voice
that is not the human language
a scream
only canines can hear

                                                I'm reaching
                                                out my hand
                                                to touch

Closer/   could you be so
  kind

                                                to not bite off
                                                my hand?

silently on the imperceptible voice
that is not the human language
again, a scream
only canines can hear

as a pin may drop
shut's the secret door within secret/　　　My bones are ice
　　　　　　　　　　　　　　　　　　　　　My marrow
　　　　　　　　　　　　　　　　　　　　　running away

Do you know what I/　　　　　　　　　strange but more
familiar

Do you remember when/　　　　　　　when my legs
could not move

You are here and there/　　　　　　　because they
were also metal

    The dancing flood lights overhead make brutal sounds of metal scraping, swaying horror flick noise shadows over benches floating in salt.

    And on the benches, a ship's bounty of sand sharks, making out with one thousand teeth.

    Beneath the sharks, Boy lost his Hanes.

    The sharks become sociopaths, unleashing their hunger.

    In the spaceship, Boy is eaten.

14.
"Those sharks are gonna die out there!"

Mother yelled from inside,
gnawing a ham and cheese.

"Your father will be back
any minute,
get cleaned up."

Boy fell from Icarus,
broke his feet upon landing,
slams into railing,
almost toppling through.

Boy followed with his eyes,
one shark.

And with a thud,
cement walkway landing,
out popped its eyes,
first and then, second.

"And throw away those goddamn fish!"

Two sharks in the pail,
walks down rental house stairs,
stomping the backyard,
on imagined stiletto clouds,
and the death of the crab.

In the trash bin,
Boy discards sun roasted bodies.

The eyes,

(meaningless)
stare back,
no gift of their own.

Boy replaces the cover,
returns to the house.

Mother lurks over,
preparations for dinner.

Dinner was sure to be one of mother's two signature dishes

>1.) Spaghetti with red sauce
>2.) Swiss steak
>>(also comes with red sauce,
>>but chunkier and with onions)

For someone transfixed on the appearance of newness,
Mother danced the edge of stain polka.

15.
Mother spoke softly on the phone

On the stairs where no one could hear,
to a friend named Rebecca.

Mother always spoke softly
to Rebecca.

16.
Swiss steak

"Take off your shoes!"
Mother's voice
to Father, returned.

Even while on vacation,
she refused to retire.

Mother removes rings
of engagement,
wedding band,
to beat sirloin tips,
with the base of her palm.

Inside a Samsonite duffel,
tube tops and hosiery,
Mother pulls out a Crockpot,
she'd brought from home.

In goes the steak,
violently abused.

Now, two onions,
quartered and sliced,
by a very dull knife.

Dump in a can
of stewed tomatoes,
two tablespoons of Wesson's,
one cup of tap water,
salt and pepper,
and garlic salt to taste.

Dial to medium,
burn the house down,
for the five and six o'clock news.

Boy has never seen Mother eat fish.

17.
1990
"fag choreography"

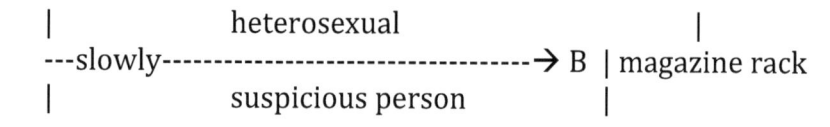

```
|              heterosexual                    |
---slowly---------------------------------→ B  | magazine rack
|              suspicious person               |
```

look left
look right
pluck International Male catalog from shelf
go right to swimwear
rip the page out
hide International Male behind US Weekly

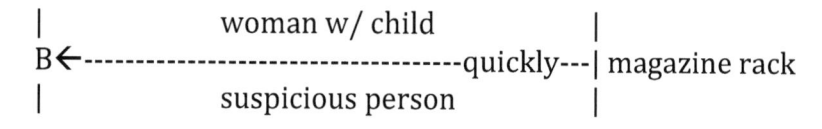

```
|              woman w/ child                  |
B←-----------------------------------quickly---| magazine rack
|              suspicious person               |
```

18.
International Meat

Swiss steak
bursting Boy's
distending belly,
nutating bowels,
consumption of anger,
of cow,
and Mother.

While jabbing around,
the beach house bedroom,
Boy notices his wrist
> *mmm...*
> a bit broken,
> a fish out of water

The remaining water wing
of a lost sea child

When dinner through, Boy runs to this room, wrestles his imitation Samsonite suitcase like Andre the Giant, found in Mother's ongoing basement sale, where nothing ever was sold.

In the pocket of Boy's Husky Straight Fits, was the contra-ban page from International Male, Summer issue, 1990.

If Boy tries
concentrate
squint eyes
bear down
look hard
get

see
image of Ahab's whale
hidden beneath
black mesh fish net

Mesh like woven shark skin

My body is not right

Not like others who live here　　　　　　　　　*while I live here*

My body
I want

The whale hides
forty seamen
in her belly.

Hard squint
harder
hardening
hardest
two whales
one becomes
toy train

My body is not right

Not like others who live here　　　　　　　　*while I dream here*

My body
I want
My body to

A single drop,
eye to paper,
mesh sticky sweet.

    My body is not

Not like the other who live here   *while I*

    Want my body
    I want
    What I cannot

A second drop,
from toy train,
makes wet,
the denim.

    my
    mine
    my own
    body is
    not

while others	*live*
while others	*lie*
while others	*lived*
while others	*like*
while	*they*

    live here
    lie here
    lie down

a round for singing:
>   row row row   *my boat*
>   row row row   *my ship*
>   *row row row*   *body slam oom-pah-pah*

light slice cut window
from the West
of rental
and leg
of Boy

The light catches a twist,
in the maverick story.

Caught on gaze,
a fresh blade,
sprouts up
through skin.

Hallelujah,
Boy thinks,
Is Jesus real?

Moss has sprung in summer.

O, excitable Summer!

Boy seizes his Huskies
from his waist to his ankles.

Newborn carpet,
to bring the tongue,
upon the leg,
a growth bath.
The cat wakes,
to lick himself.

At this moment, Boy discovers the pleasure of his own mouth upon skin.

19.
the tan, tall man,
in international shark mesh,
dark, woven

Boy fell asleep,
jeans at his ankles.

Dreaming his knees were volcanic.

Knees opened as flowers,
mutating holes,
of roses and thorns,
where buffalo nickels,
like slot machines,
shoot marrow,
til his body
turned Smucker's jam.

Weapon storage belly,
of 1001 antique lamps,
pulled from the ocean,
by his pirate Mother.

In his dreaming,
his teeth become
marble statues
of Greek gods.

The great eruption,
from under the soil,
shatters his jaw.

Marble pours
upon soil,

and where the two meet,
the figure of a tall, tan man,
known for his modeling portfolio
in the Grand International Court,
is born from a bundle of sticks.

Tall, tan man wears
a crown of fin
and shells.

His fingernails,
sharp teeth.

Boy cannot move.

       body lava
             no body
                    suppose

Eve's snake takes a breath,
where Boy tongue was once
cat bath.

Rattlesnake seizures,
shed rattlers down throat,
drawn deep into lungs.

Boy cannot breathe.

"All is not lost,"
says tall, tan man,
bearing shark teeth.

Incomparable pleasure,
the tall, tan beast,
puts his finger jaws,
into the holes,
of Boy's knees,

plucks his jelly body,
across the red lava shore,
back towards the penny arcade.

"And here you shall have
your pick,"
the tanned beast says.

Machines that steal coins,
now give mountains
of pirate's gold,
an ocean for Boy,
where Boy discovers
harsh breathing.

XX.
a three hour tour
Ocean Shitty, Jerzey

On the Good Dirty Jerzey,
Cousin Maddie hid schnapps,
in the disembodied head,
of wheelchair Barbie.

"This will bring luck,
and big blue fin to the reel,"
Maddie believed.

Jamming her tongue in the head,
Maddie flaps it violently to and fro.
    (as a broken winged bird
      caught on an electrified fence)

Now Barbie's wig
is stuck in her throat,
spent the next hour,
hacking up synthetics.

During lunch, Father daddy
put down the ham,
to play a game called crossing streams
with friends Joe, Mark and Doc.

Yellow piss sunlight,
like church stained glass,
disappears into
the murky bay.

Dear cousin Maddie,
and her black roving eyes,

spills Barbie's head booze,
on Boy's swim trunks.

"Silly Boy,
you're all wet,
put your fingers,
in my mouth."

Cousin Maddie was quick with a trick,
she could vanish your fingers in seconds.

Daddy's friend Joe caught a flounder,
as big as a pan.

Daddy's friend Mark caught a blue fin,
post-traumatically stabbed.

Daddy's daddy Doc caught crabs,
later, at night.

Boy said,
"Father, can we play
crossing streams?"

And they did,
for a few years to come,
until Mother caught wind,
and made Father's bed.

Boys never grow up,
they just become men,
who still play boy games,
after ten.

The Dirty Jerzey stayed docked,
until Desert Storm,
then went out of business,
sold at the penny arcade,

for coins.

Cousin Maddie became a nurse,
after five years in jail.

Joe took up painting,
cheap boardwalk whales.

Mark disappeared,
after hijacking a boat.

Doc got the tremens,
but never the treatment.

Father daddy keeps Polaroids
of Joe, Mark and Doc,
then Mother placed them
inside a pot,
to store in the basement,
surrounded by unused blenders,
that Father never went near.

20.
it shall pass

pocket lint

picking apples
throats
no more coins

at the remains of day

here

what is

where

the good ship
penny saver sale
to those who want
small ships
in the shape of glass houses

21.

it shall...

end of summer days
the coming of class bells

taken to sea

End of summer days,
Boy's final board walk.

Punctuation shall end,
with the closing of August,
humans wrestle with,
the temporality of joy.

Flip-flops
spiral sand bunnies
under toe

sunset

Boy walks
from rental
to ocean

visitors shred
parking passes
to make bonfires
from lit cigarettes

a child bursts

a water wing
with a fork

silence now
led zeppelins
of whiskey

the seagulls are starving

and
as
things

disappearing

as sun
       over here, sun

              setting

              Boy closer
                  over here, closer
                  to the place
                  where sand disappears
                  in lava red water
                      closer, yet
                      Boy footprints disappear
                      at shoreline
                      stares into distance
                      no more line
                      depictions
                      of cheap,
                      watercolor
                      painting

closer, still
and one foot
bathes itself
in salty sea

another step

        Boy's ankles
        in water

        what if?
        what if the shore?

        what?

        something on the
        water
        the figure of an axe
        cut the white foam
        thought race
        on the looping sea

        Boy neck deep

the figure of an a

the figure of

the figure of a

the figure of a...

fin

.../)...

You/ have sought/ me	you I have I have

Can I?	
	Can you?

Can?/	You are

silently on the imperceptible voice
that is not the human language
a scream
only sharks can hear

TAN TALL IZING	yes
	Will you?
Will I?	

                                              Will you?

Will?

                                              Won't?

that is not the human language
a scream

USE YOUR WORDS, BOY!

                                              But I am made
                                              of mesh
                                              a Boy who

cannot

                                              speak

You are the finest
of trainees
so, shall I make
you into marble
so that other boys
might pay their respects/   But, wait

that is not the human language
a scream

DO NOT INTERRUPT, BOY/ *dissed*

YOU ARE THE MAKER/ I'm?
OF MAN

silence
sans scream

                                          How will this go?

I shall take my teeth,
my godlike teeth
and begin the playful
incision.
It will be a simple moment
of pain mixed with pleasure
before you shall learn
how to receive

                                           Shall I be still?

Be what you will/
Be what you will/
Be what you will/

                                                   but
                                                   but I
                                                 clenches

And now we shall/

                                                 WAIT!
                                               I do not know

your name…

You know my name.
You gave me that.

                                                   I I I I …

You gave me the name
you wanted

                                                 I I I I…

    I am beast
    Misfit
    Tan and tall
    I make steaks
    from Boy's bellies
    nip sand at their feet

salt their cocks
and tuck them
away in lockers
I am what you made
and did not/   make?
I am what I appear
to be nothing
and everything
I spin gold
from wooden coins/   make you?
I am

Named

Drew

                                                But will?
Yes, Boy?

                                       My name

Yes... boy   *over here*

Yes, boy
I caught a fish

Over here

Slippery,
Boy

                      Now, here

Yes, Boy

              Now, here

Yes

        Now?

Now?
"Now"

will it?

and so
they sink

sinking

sinking

sinking

down

**deeper
and deeper**

As the Boy
who was now Ginger

sank deeper

deeper still

And Boy
took a bite
from the beast's side

As the beast
penetrated
a thousand
teeth
deep within

mmm
said the Boy
coiled around the shark
hold close the beast
six feet in length
but not yet
of full potential

they continued
a dance
a swim
a sinking

and where the Boy's legs,
the caudal fin.

and where the Boy's arms,
pectoral fins.

and where the Boy's round center,
muscular grey trunk.

and where the Boy's neck,
gills.

and where the Boy's fear,
a most amazing jaw.

two sharks entwined,
powering through water
like air

at sea

Made in the USA
San Bernardino, CA
04 August 2017